NO LONGER PROPERTY OF
SEATTLE PUBLIC LIBRARY

Reading

Squiggles
make letters.
Letters
make words.
Words
make stories
that fly like birds
from pages
in your book
to branches
in your brain
where they sing
into your soul
like soothing
summer rain.

Read! Read!

Rea

Rea

Read!

Poems by Amy Ludwig VanDerwater
Illustrated by Ryan O'Rourke

WORDSONG
AN IMPRINT OF HIGHLIGHTS
Honesdale, Pennsylvania

For my Henry, who loses and finds himself in books
—ALV

To my wife, Trish
—RO

For the descriptions in "Field Guide," the author consulted
A Field Guide to Hawks: North America, first edition,
by William S. Clark and Brian K. Wheeler (Houghton Mifflin Company, 1987).

Text copyright © 2017 by Amy Ludwig VanDerwater
Illustrations copyright © 2017 by Ryan O'Rourke
All rights reserved.
For information about permission to reproduce selections from this book,
contact permissions@highlights.com.

WordSong
An Imprint of Highlights
815 Church Street
Honesdale, Pennsylvania 18431
Printed in China

ISBN: 978-1-59078-975-9

Library of Congress Control Number: 2016960145

First edition
Designed by Barbara Grzeslo
The text of this book is set in Neutraface.
The illustrations were created in Adobe Photoshop.
10 9 8 7 6 5 4 3 2 1

Contents

Reading	1
Pretending	6
Cereal Box	8
Sports Page	9
Reading Time	10
I Explore	11
Maps	12
Road Signs	13
Word Collection	14
Field Guide	15
An Open Book	16
Stories	19
Double Life	20
Book Dog	21
Googling Guinea Pigs	22
Forever	24
Birthday Card	26
Magazine	27
Sunday Morning	28
Information	30
Late at Night	31
I Am a Bookmark	32
In Love	back cover

Pretending

Tracing my fingers
under each letter
I used to pretend
I could read to myself.

I didn't know how
but I didn't care.
I'd go to the library
pull from the shelf—
a rainbow of rectangles.

I longed so to read.
This was my hope.
This was my need.

Month after day
after week
I would try.
Learning to read
felt like
learning to fly.

And one day
I took off.
I was swooping
alone
over words
once confusing
but now
all my own.

6

Cereal Box

I pour my cereal into a bowl.
It makes a wind chime sound.
I pour my milk in a river of white.
I stir the two around.

And as I chew I read.
      And as I read I chew.

Recipes.
Stories.
Jokes.
Weird facts.

I read the box.
Don't you?

Sports Page

Scanning scores
studying stats
I'm checking on my team.

When they lose
I sigh.
When they win
I scream.

Who made the playoffs?
I've got to know.
Which players will stay?
Who has to go?

No need to wonder
if I'm a true fan.
I wake up and read.
That's my game plan.

Reading Time

We all read together
in the very same class
with the very same walls
and the very same floor.

We all turn pages
flip-flip-flip-flip
in the very same way
as we have before.

We all seem the same
but it's not the way it looks
for we live in different worlds
in the words of different books.

I Explore

I have lived in twenty countries.
I have walked in King Tut's tomb.
I have scuba dived through shipwrecks
as I sat here in this room.

I have stood upon a moonscape.
I have witnessed peace and war.
I have ridden a wild horse.
I'm a reader.
I explore.

Maps

Yes.
We have a GPS.
But I still like to read maps.

I like the colored lines
and all those tiny numbers.
I like the way maps fold
into themselves
like perfect beetle wings.

I like to turn maps
in air
as we turn down roads
on land.

I like to hold a whole city
crinkling
in my hands.

I like to hear
my voice command—
Turn here.
Yes.
Right here.

Road Signs

I remember staring
out my window
in the car
pointing out each *W*
each *A*
each *M*
each *R*.

The alphabet
surrounded me
marching in a line
like a secret code
for grown-ups
splashed
on every sign.

I still stare
out my window
when we're driving
down the street.
But now I know the code.
I read signs
from my backseat.

WORD COLLECTION

Knickknack
TICKTOCK
PICKPOCKET
BRIC-A-BRAC
ALLIGATOR
ELEVATOR
Hummingbird
JUMPING JACK
FLABBERGASTED
PLATYPUS
PERIWINKLE
Thumbtack
mozzarella
CINDERELLA
CENTIMETER
QUARTERBACK
BUTTERSCOTCH
SUCCOTASH
Windsock
WOLF PACK
WHIPPERSNAPPER
BELLY BUTTON
BUMBLEBEE
Knickknack

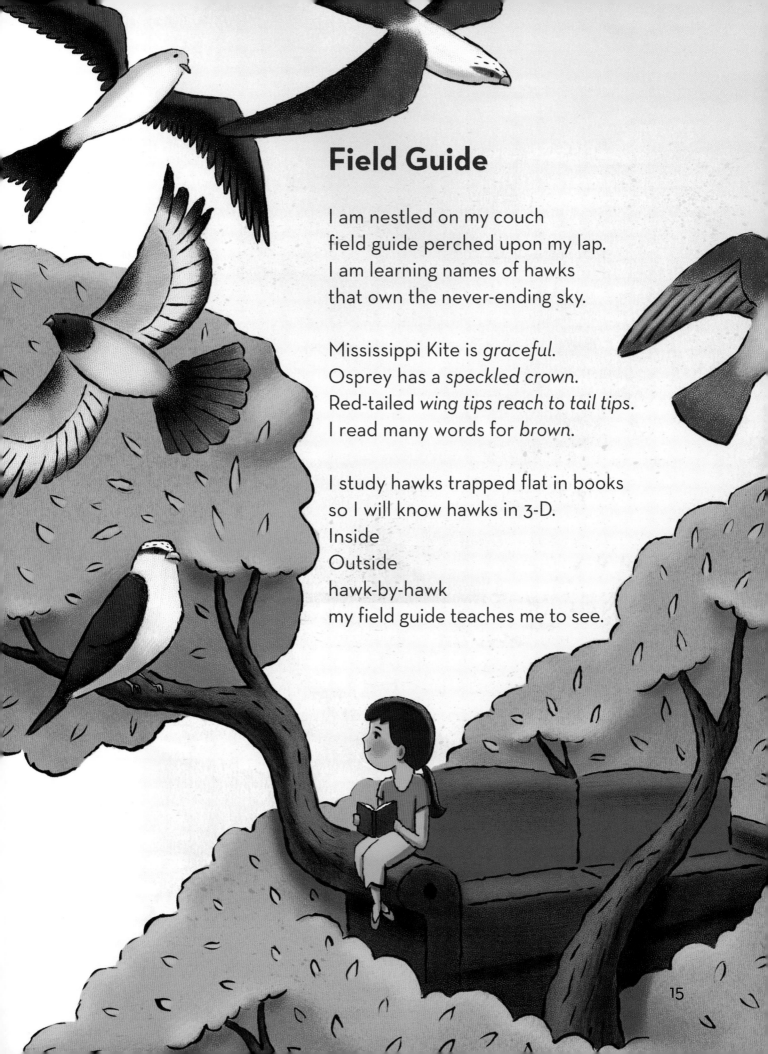

Field Guide

I am nestled on my couch
field guide perched upon my lap.
I am learning names of hawks
that own the never-ending sky.

Mississippi Kite is *graceful*.
Osprey has a *speckled crown*.
Red-tailed *wing tips reach to tail tips*.
I read many words for *brown*.

I study hawks trapped flat in books
so I will know hawks in 3-D.
Inside
Outside
hawk-by-hawk
my field guide teaches me to see.

An Open Book

An open book
will help you find
an open heart
an open mind
inside yourself
if you're inclined.
An open book
will make you kind.

Stories

I cried
when Dad read
Charlotte's Web.
I did not like that book.
I turned my face
and dried my tears
so nobody would look.

Later
when I hugged my Dad
he held me really tight.
He told me tears heal
broken hearts.
I healed my heart
that night.

She wasn't real
(of course I knew)
but *Charlotte's Web* was true.
The next year
when my Grandma died
my heart was lost
until I cried.

Charlotte taught me what to do.

Double Life

A book gives you a double life.
It builds a treehouse in your head
a haven you can climb to
when you wish to get away.

A book will always be a friend
reaching out two wordy hands
offering enchanted lands.

You can be and go
who and where
you've never been.

The cover opens.
You are born.

Let your double life begin.

Book Dog

I cannot get a real dog
but I have one in this book.
She's fluffy and she's friendly.
She's right here—take a look.

I hug my dog each time I read.
She licks me without fail.
And when I turn the pages fast
wind whisks through her tail.

My book dog meets me after school.
I sit and stay with her.
She chases through the chapters.
I pet her paper fur.

I cannot get a real dog
no matter how I plead.
But I can have a dog to love
every time I read.

Googling Guinea Pigs

Our class got a guinea pig!
A pet of our own!

Tonight at home
Mom and I Google
guinea pigs.

Read about treats.
Read about exercise.
Read about safe holding.

Tomorrow is Friday.
Cleopatra will be
our weekend guest.

I can't wait
to serve her spinach
watch her run
on dainty feet
snuggle
that royal furball
in my arms.

Forever

The author
and the illustrator
may be living
may be dead.
It doesn't matter.

Both live now
forever
in your head.

You'll be reminded
constantly
everywhere you look
that a person in your life
is like a person in a book.

You'll wander through a forest.
You'll open up a door
whispering under your breath—
I've been here once before.

Because you have.
You've read the words.
You've seen the pictures too.
Every single thing you read
becomes a part of you.

Birthday Card

Grandpa writes more
than his name on a card.

Today is my birthday.
I open Grandpa's envelope
slowly
so I don't rip his crazy doodles.

I don't look for money.
I look for words.

This year
a poem—

Fire trucks are red.
Blueberries are blue.
You're cuter than me.
I'm older than you.
Happy birthday!
Happy birthday
Sweet Child.

Just like always
I kiss his card
as I tuck it
into my secret box
stuffed with
fall leaves
letters
and love.

Magazine

Hooray!

I cheer.
It's mine!
It's here!
It comes
by mail
twelve times
each year.
I open it—
and
disappear.

Sunday Morning

I get the newspaper
first every Sunday.
Reading the comics
I laugh frame-by-frame.

I follow these friends
every week with my breakfast.
I know every character
know every name.

My parents are sleeping.
I read words and pictures.
(The cat likes lasagna.
The children play ball.)

Each square is a world
sketched alive by an artist
just for me
every Sunday.

I read them all.

Information

At dinner I ask—

*Do you know
how many pounds of skin
a person sheds by age seventy?*

My sister puts down her fork.

No.

One hundred five.

Oh.

She will not look at me.
She will not pick up her fork.

I keep eating.
I love reading.

30

Late at Night

My mom sits on my bed.
I say
I cannot sleep.
She knows my lie.

She reaches out
to touch my lamp.
The bulb is warm.
My mom knows why.

She taught me how
a story leaps
like magic
from each printed page.

I'm sure my mom
read past her bedtime
under blankets
at my age.

I Am a Bookmark

I am a bookmark
here in bed
holding the page
between
dark and light.

I am a bookmark
here in bed
between two sheets
crisp-cold
and white.

I am a bookmark
here in bed
finding my place
by reading
at night.